MAN OF THE HOUSE

A Novel by TODD STRASSER
Based on the Screenplay by JAMES ORR &
JIM CRUICKSHANK
From a Story by DAVID PECKINPAH and
RICHARD JEFFERIES
Now a Motion Picture from WALT DISNEY PICTURES

DISNEY
PRESS

New York

To Declan Kavanagh, a brave young man

Library of Congress Catalog Card Number: 94-79127
ISBN: 0-7868-4040-4

About the Author

Todd Strasser has written many award-winning novels for young and teenage readers. He speaks frequently at schools about the craft of writing and conducts writing workshops for young people. Todd lives with his wife, two children, and dog in a suburb of New York City.

O N E

Five years ago, my dad left. I was six at the time. I remember standing by the front door of our house with Mom, watching Dad back the car out of the driveway. As he backed the car into the street, he rolled down the window and waved. I waved back. Before he left, he promised to come back and visit me soon. I believed him. Looking back on it now, I guess I was being pretty dumb. He never did visit. He was never good at keeping promises.

When the car disappeared around the corner, Mom went back into the house, sat down on the living room couch, and started to cry. I went in and sat down next to her.

"We still have each other," I said. "And I'm going to

look after you for as long as I live."

Mom smiled at me through her tears and then gave me a hug. As the days passed, I realized Dad was never coming back. I guess that's when I knew I had to make sure neither one of us ever got hurt again.

After first grade Mom and I moved out of our house and into a loft apartment on the top floor of a five-story building in downtown Seattle. At first it was just this big bare space, with dust balls on the floor and about a hundred years' worth of grime on the windows. But in no time, Mom fixed it up and turned it into a home.

I hoped working on the loft would help Mom keep her mind off Dad, but it didn't. Even after she'd made the loft really nice she was still pretty sad about him leaving.

But as time passed, Mom seemed to get happier. She got a job sketching people in court. When she wasn't working we spent a lot of time walking along beaches, picking up stuff like driftwood, shells, and sea glass that we'd bring home and add to the collage we had been working on.

Our life was pretty good. We didn't think about Dad as much as when he'd first left. Mom and I had each other, and there was no one around to hurt our feelings. As far as I was concerned, it could have stayed that way forever.

But things changed when Mom started dating. Luckily, it wasn't a really big problem, because most of the guys were jerks. I don't mean to brag, but my mom deserves to be treated well. She's not only really nice, she's pretty, too. She has blond hair, sparkling eyes, and a big gleaming smile. Most of the time, I didn't like her dates, and I guess Mom didn't like them either because sooner or later each guy would go, and it would be just Mom and me again. I liked it that way, and I hoped she did, too.

But then, one morning, Mom dropped the bomb. We were in the kitchen about to have breakfast. Mom had been out the night before with the latest jerk, a goofy lawyer named Jack. Mom stood at the kitchen counter with a big smile on her face.

"What're you so happy about?" I asked as I got the yogurt out of the refrigerator. Mom and I always had breakfast together.

"Ben, honey, there's something I have to talk to you about," Mom said.

I started to get this queasy feeling in my stomach. Now that I thought about it, Mom had been in a pretty good mood for the past couple of months. She'd go around singing to herself and trying on new clothes a lot more than usual. Her hair seemed to turn a little blonder, and she was wearing more makeup.

"You know that there's a special person in my life?" she asked.

The truth was, I knew immediately who she was talking about. Jack.

This is what I knew about Jack the jerk. He lived

over in Tacoma and drove a white truck. He wore a suit and a tie most of the time, except on weekends, when he wore stuff like corduroys and crew-neck sweaters. He's tall and kind of dorky, with a goofy face and a receding hairline. Sometimes he wore jeans, but if he did, they'd usually have a *crease* in them. To me, that says it all.

Mom met him in court. She was drawing pictures of the people he was trying to send to jail. He's a U.S. attorney, so he gets to deal with real criminals like kidnappers and drug dealers. Recently, he sent a big drug dealer to the Federal Correctional Facility in Sheridan, Oregon, for fifty years. It was even written about in the newspapers.

I hadn't paid that much attention to him, since I figured it was only a matter of time before Mom erased his number from her phone book. Only now that I thought more about it, it seemed like he'd lasted a lot longer than any of the previous jerks.

"Things have gotten pretty serious," Mom said.

That queasy feeling in my stomach was getting worse. "You're not getting married," I said. Didn't she learn her lesson with Dad?

"Not yet," Mom said.

For a second I felt relieved, then I realized what she'd said. "Not *yet*?"

"We're going to live together first," Mom said.

"You and Jack the jerk? *Live* together?" I repeated, hoping that I was mistaken.

Mom almost smiled, but then she got serious.

"Don't call him that, hon. But yes, me and Jack. Or I should say, Jack and I."

"What about me?" I asked.

"You'll live with us, too, silly."

"Where?"

"Here."

Jack the jerk was moving in with us? That sense of dread in my stomach grew even bigger. I pushed my chair back. "Excuse me, I think I'm going to hurl."

"Now, Ben," my mother said. "At least give him a chance."

"Aren't you worried he's going to do the same thing Dad did?" I asked. "Like split and leave you miserable?"

"No, I really don't think he will," Mom said. "He's not like your dad."

I still didn't like it. "You hardly know this guy. What if he turns out to be a serial killer and wants to boil our heads in acid?"

Mom smiled. "You're stretching, Benjamin."

"Hey, it could happen," I said.

"Look, this is only a trial period," Mom said. "Jack's going to keep his own apartment, so if it doesn't work out . . . well, then he'll go back to his place, and you and I will go back to the way things were."

"Do you know that he actually irons his jeans?" I asked.

Mom sighed. "Ben, try to be optimistic."

I just stared at her in disbelief.

T W O

The day before Jack moved in, Mom straightened the place up a little. "Making room for Jack," she said. She put away a lot of half-finished paintings and art supplies that had been lying around. I was worried that she might want to put away the big seashore collage we'd been working on together. I was glad when she decided to leave it leaning against the wall.

At one point, Mom and I stood together and looked at it.

"Know what I noticed about our collages?" I asked.

Mom shook her head.

"They always sort of start out like circles, but they never end like a circle."

"I've noticed that, too," Mom said.

"Why do you think that is?" I asked.

"Sometimes I think it's because a circle represents something that's complete," she said. "And I don't feel complete."

"How come?"

"Because our family isn't complete."

"Because I don't have a father?" I guessed.

Mom nodded. "But you know what? Sometimes I think it has nothing to do with that. Sometimes I think I'm just worried that if we don't change the collage, it'll end up looking like a happy face."

"That sounds better," I said.

The next morning, bright and early, before I had even finished my breakfast, the buzzer rang. "That's him," Mom said as she raced out the door and took the elevator downstairs. I went over to the window and looked down at the street. Jack was just getting out of his truck.

I was instantly filled with dread. I couldn't believe it was really happening. How could that *total stranger* just move in with us?

I watched Mom come out the front door of our building and give Jack a hug. Then when they started to kiss, I had to look away. When I looked back, Mom was unloading boxes from the car and giving them to Jack. After a while, he had so many boxes in his arms it looked like he was going to topple over. Then he started to teeter, and Mom had to grab him by the shirt and aim him in the right direction. I secretly hoped he'd trip over the front steps. Pretty soon I heard the door of the loft open. Jack stumbled in under all those boxes and put them down on the floor.

"Hey, Ben," he said with a big goofy smile.

I gave him a little wave and looked back out the window. After a moment, I heard him walk back to the elevator. As soon as the elevator doors closed, I went over to examine the boxes he'd left. Each one was carefully marked with the contents: Files, Computer, Pillow . . .

Pillow? The guy had to bring his own pillow? *Dork!*

One box was labeled Law Texts, and because it was open, I looked in. Inside was a black leather-bound book with the title *Criminal Psychology: Profiles of Serial Killers.*

I knew it! I quickly looked in the index under Sturges, Jack's last name. Nope, no serial killers by that name. Of course, that didn't mean Jack wasn't a serial killer. It only meant that he hadn't been caught yet.

The elevator doors in the hall opened again, and I quickly put the book back in the box. Jack and Mom came in carrying more stuff.

"Ben, do you think you could give us a hand?" Mom asked.

A hand? Help that dork move into our home? She *had* to be kidding.

"I'd like to, Mom," I said, flopping down on a chair

in the living room. "But I've got a sore back. The doctor said I shouldn't do any heavy lifting."

Mom gave me a look to let me know I wasn't fooling her. "Then maybe you could do something light," she said. "Like make room for Jack's things in the closet under the stairs."

I looked at her in shock. "But that's where we keep all the stuff we collect from the beach."

"We'll put it somewhere else for the time being," Mom said.

"But it's important stuff," I said.

"It'll be fine if we put it somewhere else."

My worst fear was coming true. Jack was moving in, and nothing else mattered. Meanwhile, he was standing there teetering under another mountain of boxes in his arms.

"It's okay," he said. "I don't need to put my stuff away this instant. I can just hold it. It's more convenient if I need to get anything."

He always talked that way. Kind of goofy, but wise guy at the same time. So even if you thought he was being sarcastic, you couldn't say anything because he could easily deny it.

"No, no, it's no trouble," Mom said, then glared at me. "Is it, Benjamin?"

Great. Now she put me on the spot. "No, it's no trouble," I muttered, getting up. I went over to the stairs and opened the closet door. There, I'd done something. Jack could dump his stuff in the closet for all I cared.

"Thanks, Benny!" Jack shouted sarcastically as I walked away. "I really appreciate it."

That was it. I marched right over to Mom. "You know I hate being called Benny."

"I'll tell him, hon," Mom promised.

It was time to disappear into my room. That was one place Jack wasn't going to take over.

T H R E E

Things were going from bad to worse. After Jack finished moving in, he said he had to take a shower. I could hear his tone-deaf singing coming from the bathroom.

"Someone dying?" I asked Mom, who was in her bedroom, moving things around to make more room for you-know-who.

"It's just Jack," she said. "He sings in the shower."

"You know, I've been waiting to get in there for about an hour," I said.

"An hour?" Mom raised a skeptical eyebrow.

"Okay, five minutes," I admitted. "How long's he going to be?"

Mom shrugged. "Why don't you ask him?"

That wasn't a bad idea. I went over to the bathroom and knocked. "Jack, you going to be in there all night?" I called.

No answer. He couldn't hear me over his singing. I decided to get his attention another way.

I went to the kitchen, reached over the sink, and turned the hot water faucet on full force.

In the bathroom, Jack suddenly changed his tune. *"Whoa! Hey! Yeow!"*

I couldn't help smiling to myself. I turned off the hot water and headed back toward the bathroom. Jack came out just as I got there. He'd wrapped a towel around his waist. His head was covered with shampoo foam.

"What happened to the hot water?" he asked with a shiver.

"It's an old building," I said. "Sometimes it just cuts out. You never know."

Before Jack could get back into the bathroom, I slid past him and locked the door.

"Ben?" Jack knocked on the bathroom door. "Ben! Hey, c'mon, I'm covered with soap!"

The bathroom was all steamed up. I took a towel and wiped the fog off the mirror on the medicine cabinet.

"What're you doing?" I heard my mother asking Jack outside the bathroom.

"Dripping," I heard Jack reply. "Ben locked me out

of the bathroom. You don't think he did it on purpose, do you?"

"Of course not," I heard my mother say. "I'll get you a towel."

Inside the bathroom I opened the medicine cabinet and found that my toothpaste and toothbrush were gone. The cabinet was filled with deodorant, aftershave lotion, cologne, talcum powder, mouthwash, and about a dozen other strange bottles and containers full of scented stuff. Jack must have thought he smelled like a skunk.

A bunch of pill bottles lined one shelf, and I checked out a few. They were all for allergies. Great, the guy smelled bad and had allergies, too! This was supposed to be my adult male role model?

"Hey, Mom!" I called out. "Where's my toothpaste? I can't find it!"

Mom didn't answer, so I opened the bathroom door and came across a truly gross scene. Mom and Jack were standing in the living room kissing while the shampoo foam on Jack's head oozed down his neck and shoulders.

"Excuse me," I said. "Do you guys *have* to do that?"

That broke them up. Mom turned slightly red and Jack grinned.

"Oops, sorry," he said. "I just can't resist a pretty girl. You know how it is, right, buddy?"

"I'm eleven," I informed him. "I hate girls."

"Right, of course." Jack winked. "I used to be

eleven myself. I know exactly what you mean. Cooties, right?"

"Yeah, right. Cooties." I rolled my eyes. What was with this guy?

"Well, now that the coast's clear." Jack went back into the bathroom and closed the door. I turned to Mom.

"I can't find my toothpaste," I said. "I can't find anything. All my bathroom stuff's gone."

"It's not gone," she said. "I put it in the floor cabinet."

"Why'd you do that?"

"Because Jack's much taller than you," she said. "It makes more sense for his stuff to be up in the medicine chest." Mom looked impatiently at me. "It's not going to kill you to keep your toothpaste in that cabinet."

I pouted.

"Don't give me that face," she said. "We're all going to have to make a few adjustments."

She went back into the bedroom, and I stood outside the bathroom and waited for Jack to come out. I wasn't sure I agreed with Mom. So far it looked like I was the only one making any adjustments.

Then the bathroom door opened, and Jack came out and yawned. "Well, I'm beat. I'm going to turn in. See you in the morning, Benny."

I felt my jaw clench.

"Er, I meant, Ben," Jack quickly corrected himself. "See you in the morning, *Ben*."

F O U R

Thunk! Sometime in the middle of the night I was awakened by the sound of a crash downstairs. A few moments later I heard whispering. I got out of bed and went to the door. Downstairs, in the shadows of the streetlights outside, I could see Mom and Jack huddled outside Mom's bedroom door.

"What's going on?" I asked.

"Nothing!" they answered together.

Yeah, right, I thought. "Then why are you whispering?"

"We didn't want to wake you, hon," Mom said.

"I heard a noise," I said.

"Oh, that was just me doing a little late-night

skateboarding," Jack said. "I was on my way to the bathroom when I tripped on this darn skateboard. I wonder who it belongs to."

He was being sarcastic again. Jack limped toward the bathroom, and I looked down at Mom. I just didn't get it. Why did she have to get involved with this guy?

"Good night, *Mother*," I said.

"Good night, sweetheart," Mom said, and closed her bedroom door.

The next morning, I woke up to the smell of smoke. Scared that the building was on fire, I jumped out of bed, pulled on my pants, and ran out of my room. The smoke seemed to be coming from the kitchen.

I went downstairs. What a mess! The kitchen counter was covered with broken, dripping eggs, burned English muffins, and melted butter. Smoke was billowing out of the toaster and from a frying pan on the stove.

Jack was standing in the kitchen, covered in guck. He was holding a dish towel over the top of the blender and trying to reach the knobs on the stove with his foot.

"What are you doing?" I asked.

Jack spun around and gave me that stupid smile. "'Morning, Ben! I couldn't sleep for some reason, so I thought I'd get up early and make breakfast."

"Mom and I always make breakfast together," I said matter-of-factly.

"Well, I wanted to show you that I'm part of the team now," Jack said. "Uh, listen, think you could do me a favor and turn down the stove?"

I went over to the stove and turned down the flame under the burning frying pan. When the smoke cleared a bit I could see something in the pan that resembled eggs. "What *is* that?" I asked.

"Eggs Benedict à la Sturges," Jack said proudly.

"Eggs what?"

"Poached eggs and a slice of ham on English muffins, topped with hollandaise sauce," Jack said. He looked up. "Most of which is on the ceiling."

I looked up and saw yellow sauce splattered all over the ceiling above the blender. Mom was going to have a fit.

"And then the à la Sturges part," Jack said, dumping a spoonful of red glop on the eggs. "Caviar."

Fish eggs, I thought. This had to be the most disgusting breakfast I'd ever seen.

"Does the word *cholesterol* mean anything to you?" I asked.

"It's not like I eat this every morning," Jack replied. "This is sort of a celebration."

Than I noticed that our plastic recycling bins were out of order and that there were eggshells in the paper-only can.

"How about the word *recycle*?" I asked. "You put the eggshells in with the paper."

Jack scowled. "Oh. I thought it was strange that you had four different garbage cans."

I explained that one was for glass, one for metal, one for paper, and one for organic waste.

"Hey, no problemo," Jack said, reaching into the paper-only can and taking out the eggshells.

"Good morning, you two," Mom said, hurrying into the kitchen. "Mmmm, something smells good."

The kitchen was a wreck. Normally, she would have had a fit. But she was *in love*. So she smiled like nothing was wrong and said, "Gee, what happened here?"

"I made eggs Benedict!" Jack announced proudly.

"He's trying to kill us with fat," I said, heading into the living room, where it was less smokey. Couldn't she see what a *dork* this guy was?

"Ben and I usually have granola, yogurt, and sliced fruit in the morning," Mom explained.

"Oh, okay, fine." Jack looked a little disappointed. "I'll just dump this stuff in with the other organic material." He shoveled the eggs into the organic trash. "Now, how about I whip up some granola, sliced fruit, and a little yogurt? That okay?"

"Don't bother," I said, heading back upstairs. "I'll pick up something on the way to school."

Upstairs I got dressed for school. I left my door slightly open so I could hear what they were saying.

"I guess Ben and I aren't getting off to a great start, huh?" Jack said.

"Well, see, Ben and I make breakfast together every morning," Mom explained. "It's one of our routines.

I'll make up a list so this doesn't happen again."

Good luck, I thought.

F I V E

I went to a public school about five blocks away from home. One of my best friends was a kid named Monroe. When I came out of the lunch line that afternoon, I found him sitting at our regular table.

"Whoa, someone sure is hungry," he said as I sat down with a tray piled high with salad, fruit, and bread.

"How's it going, dude," I said.

"Don't they feed you at home?" Monroe asked.

"I skipped breakfast. My mom's boyfriend took over the kitchen, and I walked out in protest."

"Oh, right, the dude moved in this weekend,"

Monroe said. "I could have told you that was going to happen. First they take over the bathroom, and then they take over the kitchen."

He caught me by surprise. That was *exactly* what had happened!

"Next he takes over the sofa and the TV," Monroe said. "My advice to you is to get rid of the guy *now*."

"How?" I asked, throwing my hands into the air.

"Easy. Just convince your mother he's going to be a lousy stepfather. I got rid of two of my mom's boyfriends that way."

Just then I recalled how Mom had said that if it didn't work out for me, it wouldn't work out for her, either. But trying to convince her that Jack wasn't going to work out for me seemed really complicated.

"I don't know if I can do it," I said. "My mom's trapped inside this huge love bubble. She's not thinking clearly."

"Of course not," Monroe said. "It's your job to *help* her think clearly."

After lunch, on our way to class, Monroe started talking about my situation again.

"I'm telling you, Ben," he said, "you'd better do something fast because it's been my experience that the longer a mom lives with a guy, the harder it is for a kid to get rid of him."

I was thinking about that when we suddenly heard a muffled voice and a loud banging sound. It was coming from *inside* a locker.

"Hello?" a voice said. "Can someone get me out of here?"

Monroe and I stopped in front of the locker and looked at each other. "Is someone in there?" I asked.

"Can you please let me out?" the voice pleaded. *"Please?"*

"What's the combination?" I asked.

"Thirty-eight, twenty-four, thirty-six."

I did the combination and pulled open the locker door. Inside was a white kid wearing Native American clothing—moccasins and a beaded vest.

"Wow, thanks," he gasped. "It was really tight in there. I'm Norman Bronski, by the way."

The kid held out his hand. Monroe and I shook it and introduced ourselves.

"Don't you know you're supposed to be on the *outside* of the locker before you close it?" Monroe asked jokingly.

"Some big kids stuffed me in there," Norman explained. "They were making fun of me."

"Does that happen a lot?" I asked, staring at his outfit.

Norman nodded. "Like everyday."

"Maybe that dorky-looking getup has something to do with it," I said.

"It's got everything to do with it. I'm an Indian Guide," Norman said.

"A what?" Monroe and I both said at the same time.

"The YMCA Indian Guides is a program designed

to foster understanding and companionship between fathers and sons," Norman explained.

Just as Norman finished talking, I felt an idea taking shape in my head.

Brinnnng! The bell rang.

"Well, nice talking with you, Cochise," Monroe said. "But we've got to be going. Come on, Ben."

"Hold up a second," I said, turning to Norman. "Tell me something. Do the fathers have to dress like Indians, too?"

"Oh, sure," Norman said. "My dad wears a huge headdress with a lot of feathers on it."

"Sounds really exciting," Monroe said sarcastically, tugging on my arm. "Come on, Ben, let's go."

"How do you join up?" I asked.

Norman reached into his locker and handed me a brochure. "Everything you need to know is here. You and your dad should join. Our tribe's always looking for new members. Anyway, nice meeting you guys. And if you happen to come by this way tomorrow, could you check and see if I'm stuffed in my locker again?"

"Sure thing." Monroe and I headed down the hall while I read all about how to become an Indian Guide. The more I read, the better it sounded.

"You serious about this Indian stuff?" Monroe asked.

"Of course not," I said with a mischievous grin. "The whole thing's totally twilight zone. But that's the point."

Monroe frowned. "You lost me, Ben."

"My mom's boyfriend is trying to bond with me, right? He feels he has to prove that he can be a great stepfather to me."

"So?" Monroe said, still a bit confused.

"So I pretend being an Indian Guide is what I've always wanted to do," I said. "He'll go to a couple of meetings, hate it, and want to quit. Then I can tell my mom he's blocking my development as a child. Which, by the way, my mother takes very seriously. And then she'll give him the boot."

"But how do you know he'll hate being an Indian Guide?"

"Are you serious?" I said, opening the brochure and showing him a photo of a bunch of dweeb kids and their fathers all dressed up like Tonto. "Look at these bozos. A guy would have to be totally weird not to hate this."

Monroe raised his eyebrows and said, "You know, it just might work."

SIX

I could tell Jack kept waiting for me to change my mind. But on the night of the Indian Guide pow-wow, I still wanted to go. It was at Norman Bronski's house. On our way over to the meeting, I could see Jack still wasn't comfortable with the idea of becoming an Indian Guide.

"I never knew you had an interest in Native Americans," he said, sounding puzzled.

"Oh, yeah," I said. "Always."

"I read in the brochure that they actually eat nuts and berries," Jack said. "I would have thought you ate enough of that stuff at breakfast."

"I can never get enough," I said.

"And they make stuff like furry refrigerator

magnets. I didn't know the Indians were into that," Jack said with a laugh.

"They've had to adjust with the times," I said.

When we got to Norman's house, his father, Chet, let us inside and led us downstairs to their basement rec room, where we joined the other fathers and sons. We all sat on the floor in a circle wearing Indian stuff, banging drums, and chanting. In the center of the circle was a fake fire made out of orange paper with a lightbulb glowing in the middle.

Chet Bronski was a high school shop teacher. He was wearing a full Indian war bonnet and war paint on his face. After we banged the drums for a while, he raised his arms in the air.

"Great Spirit," he said, "we ask you to bless this tribal gathering. And to also bless our tribal brothers gathering in thousands of homes all across this great land."

Then he led us in the Indian Guides song:

Pals forever! Pals forever!
That's our slogan, that's our song.
Boys are stronger, dads feel younger
When they take the boys along!
Moms are for it, Dads adore it.
And the boys all think it's fine!
Pals forever, pals forever.
As Indian Guides we'll all have good times!

Everyone clapped and cheered. Even Jack, who looked like he couldn't believe he was really doing it.

"All right, Guides!" Norman's father said. "As Chief Running Horse of the Minotauk, it is my very special pleasure to welcome two new members to the tribe. Please join me in a big Guide welcome to Jack and Ben!"

Everyone clapped and cheered for us. Jack gave them a little nod. I'm sure he thought this was the craziest thing he'd ever seen.

Norman's father gave us the peace sign. "Hey-ha-wa-ya, Ben. Hey-ha-wa-ya, Jack."

"Fine, thanks," Jack said. "How are you?"

"No, no." Chet shook his head, and the feathers on his headdress ruffled. "Hey-ha-wa-ya is the official greeting of the Minotauk. Just a little something we made up."

"Oh, well, it's very catchy," Jack said in his sarcastic way. "I like it."

"It's just our way of saying welcome, relax, and have a good time," Chet explained. "You're among friends."

"Great," Jack said. "I feel comfortable already." Then he turned to me. "How about you, Ben? Feeling comfortable?"

"Comfortable doesn't *begin* to describe how I feel," I said. I felt great watching cool Mr. Jack squirm through this. There was no way he was going to last more than two meetings.

27

"Okay, let's start tonight's meeting with a story," Chet said. "Who's got a story to tell?"

One of the fathers raised his hand. His name was Red, and he worked for the Department of Motor Vehicles. His son's name was Hank.

"Yes, Silver Fox?" Chet asked.

"I believe it's customary at this juncture for new members to pick names for each other," Red said.

"Ah, yes," said Chet. "Once again Silver Fox nails the chief on a point of order."

"I believe it's important to follow procedure," Red explained to the rest of us. "To set an example for the youngsters."

"Silver Fox is the tribal secretary," Chet said, holding up a thick paperback book. "He's memorized the whole Guide manual word for word."

"Took me about six months," Red said proudly. I was starting to get the feeling this wasn't someone who I wanted to give me my driving test.

"Fathers and sons picking names for each other is an important Indian Guide ritual," Chet told us. "As you know, I'm Running Horse, and my son, Norman, is Dark Eagle."

"So every name has something to do with animals?" Jack guessed.

"Right, or nature," Chet said. "So why don't you pick a name for Ben."

"Sure. How about, uh, Little Wing?"

"Good name!" Chet agreed enthusiastically. "Good

song, too! Jimi Hendrix. I got the album, *Axis: Bold as Love*. Ben's tribal name will be Little Wing."

Everyone clapped and cheered.

"Now, Little Wing," Chet said to me. "Pick a name for Jack. Something that tells us how you feel about him."

How I felt about him? I had to think for a moment. Then it hit me. "How about Squatting Dog?"

Jack stared at me with raised eyebrows. "That's the best you could come up with?"

"Well, yeah," I said innocently.

"Good name!" Chet cheered. "Funny name! Minotauk like a sense of humor. From now on, Jack's tribal name will be Squatting Dog."

Everyone clapped and cheered. Then it was on to storytelling time. Everyone wanted to tell a story, but a father named Lloyd went first. His Indian name was Silent Thunder. Instead of speaking, he stood up and began to twist and turn and bend in bizarre ways. All the Guides laughed and nodded and seemed to understand this body language, but Jack and I didn't have a clue about what he was doing. Then Chet leaned toward us and whispered, "Silent Thunder is a circus performer. He likes to express himself without words."

"Oh." Jack grinned. "I thought we were playing charades."

"No, no," Chet said. "But I think he makes himself understood pretty well, don't you think?"

Jack nodded. "Oh, absolutely. I'm following right along."

I couldn't help chuckling for a second. I was getting used to Jack's humor and realized he *was* sort of funny. But I still felt like I had to get rid of him.

Lloyd finished his act, and everyone clapped and cheered. I was starting to get the feeling they'd clap and cheer even if someone blew his nose.

"That was a very good lesson, Silent Thunder," Chet said. "Did all you Little Guides learn from it?"

"Yeah," all the other kids cheered.

"Great." Chet clapped his hands together. "Now let's have some fun. Who's up for a game of scrambled moccasins?"

"Point of order, Chief." Red raised his hand again.

"Yes, Silver Fox?" Chet said with a sigh. He was obviously getting tired of all these points of order.

"I believe we played scrambled moccasins last week," Red said. "Since we've agreed to vary the games from week to week, it's either potato bowling or pass the grapefruit."

We ended up playing potato bowling, which entailed rolling potatoes into the center of a circle drawn on newspaper. Of course, the whole thing was totally absurd, since there was no way we could get the potatoes to roll straight. But the other fathers and sons all acted like it was really fun.

Then, during the crafts portion of the evening, we actually made furry refrigerator magnets! Jack looked pretty foolish while making his magnet. At the end of the gathering, the Guides all agreed to have a camp-out on the upcoming Saturday night. I was certain that if I insisted we be Indian Guides long enough, it would drive Jack crazy. That is, if *I* didn't go bonkers first.

SEVEN

The next day after school, Monroe and I went to the video arcade down the block. We played a totally awesome game with these steroid-fed gladiators boxing each other into unrecognizable blobs.

"You were right," I said as I played. "As soon as I said I liked the Indian Guides, Jack said he liked them, too."

On the screen, one gladiator punched the other so hard that his eyeballs bounced to the ground and rolled away.

"Yes!" I shouted.

"But Jack really hates it, right?" Monroe said.

"Totally," I said, laughing. "You should have been

32

there. We all had to play this game where you roll potatoes on the floor."

"No way." Monroe turned to me in surprise.

"Way," I said. "I swear! And at the end we all had to join hands and sing 'Kum-ba-yah.' "

Monroe's eyes widened. "How can *you* stand it, Ben?"

"I can't," I said. "But I'm hoping Jack will break first. There's a dopey camp-out on Saturday night. We're all going to sleep in someone's backyard.

"It's perfect," I continued. "Jack even has trouble sleeping in a bed. He'll never get any rest."

"You are bad, Ben," Monroe said with a grin.

"Just wait," I said. "I told Jack that all the other fathers were dressing up like authentic Indians. So he's going to go out and rent a whole Indian costume just to show me how enthusiastic he is about the Guides."

"Are the other fathers dressing up like Indians, too?" Monroe asked.

"Of course not," I said with a mischievous smile.

Monroe laughed. "You aren't bad, dude, you are wicked!"

On the screen, one of the gladiators raised his bulging arms in triumph. The other lay on his back, jerking spasmodically.

"Yes!" I shouted, victoriously.

The next night I heard Jack complaining to my mother about the Native American costume he had rented. He had been so busy at work that he had to call a tailor to come to his office and fit him for the costume. Right in the middle of the fitting, Jack's boss came in with a U.S. senator, who had a fit when he saw Jack, a top U.S. attorney, wearing Native American garb. Jack said his boss was really annoyed. I felt a little bad about that. Sure, I wanted Jack out of my home, but I didn't want him to get fired, too.

When Saturday night finally came, Jack got dressed up like an Indian, and we went over to Norman's house. As we got out of the car and were walking to the front door, I noticed that a black sedan was parked across the street with two mean-looking guys sitting in it. It was strange because I had seen that same car parked outside our apartment building earlier. But I didn't think too much about it because I was more interested in making a fool of Jack.

As we walked into the backyard, Jack's face turned bright red when he saw that the other fathers weren't dressed like Indians. Instead, they were all dressed in street clothes and just wore their Guide headbands.

"Gee, Squatting Dog," Chet said. "I forgot to tell you. We don't usually get all dressed up, except on special occasions."

"Oh, well, that's okay," Jack said, giving me a cold glance. "I just happened to have this lying around my closet anyway."

"Well, it looks great," Chet said, slapping him on the shoulder.

Meanwhile, it was time for us to put on our war paint. The container of face paint had a warning on the label that stated it might irritate sensitive skin. I didn't bother to tell that to Jack.

"Hey, Jack," I said. "You need to get your face painted like everyone else."

He sat down, and I started to paint his face.

"I thought you said all the other fathers were going to be wearing Indian costumes," he said under his breath.

"I guess I misunderstood," I replied innocently. "Hope you're not mad at me."

"No, no," Jack said quickly. "I'm sure it was just an honest mistake."

"Yeah," I said, painting a bright yellow happy face on his forehead.

Suddenly Jack straightened up as if he'd thought of something. "Wait a minute, what kind of paint are you using? I have to be careful."

"It's not really paint," I said, "just watercolor."

"Oh, good," Jack relaxed. "I have a tendency to break out."

"Hey, don't worry," I said with a smirk. "I checked the label."

"Time to play pass the grapefruit," Chet yelled.

We got into two lines. The fathers had to get on their knees, and the kids got to stay on their feet. The object of the game was to race down to the other end of the yard and back with a grapefruit tucked under your chin and your hands behind your back.

Jack and Chet were the first in each line. Red put a grapefruit under each of their chins and reminded them of the rules.

"On your marks, get set, go!" he shouted.

Chet and Jack started across the yard on their knees with the grapefruits under their chins. While I stood there and watched them, Norman whispered, "I think my dad's been talking to your dad about being a stepfather. I mean, he knows he might marry your mom."

"We're not going to be thrown out of the Indian Guides, are we?" I asked horrified. I was afraid that I would have to start all over again in order to get rid of Jack. I didn't think I had the energy.

"Naw," Norman reassured me. "Chet's my stepdad, too."

"No kidding," I said.

"Yeah," Norman said, and then whispered. "Believe me, there's no way I'd be an Indian Guide if it wasn't for him."

Down at the other end of the yard, Jack's grapefruit slipped out from under his chin, and as he tried to pick it up off the ground, I watched him fall flat on his face!

"Remember!" Red shouted as he ran toward them. "No hands!"

It was fun for me to watch Jack squirm around on the ground. I figured after that, he could look forward to a nice long night of sleeplessness on the cold hard ground. If that didn't get him to quit the Indian Guides, nothing would.

EIGHT

I figured that Jack would quit the next morning, but it wasn't until the following night after work that the good news finally came. Jack was in a pretty bad mood all through dinner. His face had a deep red rash in the shape of a happy face from where I'd applied the war paint. Later on, as I was getting ready for bed, I listened while Jack and Mom talked downstairs.

I heard him tell Mom that the Salish Indian tribe was suing the government over indigenous land rights and that they had a well-known Native American lawyer named Leonard Red Crow. Jack complained that he had to show up in court with the rash on his face—and everyone thought it was war paint.

I could hear Mom chuckle.

But Jack wasn't laughing. His boss had gotten so mad at him that he took him off the case for being politically incorrect.

There was this long silence, and then finally I heard Jack take a deep breath. "Well, I hate to say this, but being an Indian Guide just isn't going to work."

"Oh boy." Mom sounded pretty disappointed. "Ben's not going to be happy. He really seems to be enjoying it."

"Well, then you tell me what to do," Jack said. "I can either be a U.S. attorney or an Indian Guide, but I can't be both. You can see my point, can't you?"

"Yes," Mom said. "I just don't know how we're going to tell him."

It was time for me to be melodramatic.

"Nobody has to tell me anything," I shouted, coming out of my room. "I heard the whole thing!"

Jack and Mom looked stunned as I stomped down the stairs into the living room.

"I knew this was going to happen," I said with a great big pout on my face. I pointed to Jack. "Just when I was beginning to have fun and make new friends, *he* wants to quit!"

Mom glanced at Jack and then quickly looked back at me. "Oh, sweetheart, there are plenty of other things you and Jack can do together."

"Sure!" Jack piped up. "We can go to baseball games and movies and—"

"Yeah, yeah," I cut him off. "Until you get tired of *them* and quit!" I turned to Mom. "I *told* you he was going to be just like dad!"

I'd completed my performance. Now it was time to head back upstairs and let Mom and Jack think about it.

"Wait a minute, Ben," Jack called behind me. "That's not fair!"

Hadn't he ever heard the phrase "All's fair in love and war"? I headed toward my room and slammed the door behind me but then quietly opened it again so that I could listen to what they were saying downstairs.

"I was afraid this was going to happen," Mom said.

"Don't you think he's overreacting a little?" Jack asked. "I mean, this is just about those stupid Indian Guides."

"No, it's *not* just about those stupid Indian Guides," Mom snapped irritably. "It's about you and Ben. I told you this was going to be a difficult adjustment for Ben to make. But you said, oh, no, you were an expert. You had books on the subject."

She sounded angry. It sounded like there wasn't going to be a honeymoon.

"I'm doing the best I can," Jack said.

"Well, that doesn't seem to be good enough, does it?" Mom replied sharply.

Everything was quiet. Then Jack said, "What is *that* supposed to mean?"

"It means . . . ," Mom began, but then her voice softened. "I don't know," she said. "Maybe this is all happening too soon. Maybe I should wait until Ben is older and able to handle this better. Maybe then we'd *all* be able to handle this better."

I could hear her shut her bedroom door.

All right, Mom! I pumped my fist. Throw the dork out of here!

I closed my bedroom door and went over to the phone and called Monroe.

"Hello?" Monroe answered.

"Dude, it's Ben," I said excitedly. "I did it, Monroe! I broke the love bubble."

"You did?" Monroe asked.

"Yeah, and not a minute too soon," I said. "I don't know how much longer I could have put up with those Indian geeks."

"So he quit being an Indian Guide, huh?" Monroe said.

"Yeah, he quit," I said. "Then I went into my upset-child act. Then he and Mom started to fight, and she said she was going to wait until I was older and better able to handle it."

"Is he still there?" Monroe asked.

"Yeah, but he's history," I said. "He'll be back in Tacoma by tomorrow."

When I got off the phone, I thought I heard

someone standing outside my bedroom. Could it have been Jack? Had he been listening?

NINE

I felt great the next day. I bladed to school, had a
terrific day, and then bladed home. I had no
doubt that Jack would be gone. I got to my building, unlaced the blades, and went up in the elevator.
I got off on our floor, pushed open the door, and
cruised in.

Jack was still there, and he was sitting on the couch
next to Mom.

"Ben," he said with a big smile. "One of the great
men! We've been waiting for you!"

I'm not sure I did a good job of hiding my disap-
pointment. "What's going on? What are you doing
here?"

"Jack doesn't want to quit the Indian Guides after all," Mom said. "Isn't that wonderful, sweetheart?"

No, it wasn't wonderful. In fact, it was a nightmare. "You're kidding," I said.

"Absolutely not," Jack said. "And to prove it, I want you to meet someone."

Huh? Now what? Jack pointed to the chair where a man in a suit was sitting.

"Ben, this is Leonard Red Crow," Jack said. "Leonard, this is Ben."

The man stood up and raised his hand. "How."

"Excuse me?" I said. This *had* to be a joke. "Did you say 'How'?"

"That's Indian humor," Red Crow said.

"Leonard's the chief of the Salish Indian tribe," Jack explained. "He also happens to be an attorney. But don't hold that against him."

"So Jack tells me you're the one who's responsible for that rash on his face," Red Crow said.

"Oh, uh, it was sort of an accident," I said.

"Well, I owe you one, kid," Red Crow said with a smile. "Thanks to you and that rash, I won the case."

"Gee, uh, great." I didn't know if I was supposed to be glad for him or not.

"You're probably wondering why Leonard is here," Jack said. "Well, I've asked him to help us make the Minotauk the best tribe in the whole Indian Guide nation. What do you think of that?"

Still in shock, I said, "Uh, great."

"It's probably impossible, but I love a challenge," Red Crow added. "Besides, I can use the beads and trinkets Jack offered me."

Jack, Mom, and I glanced at each other uncertainly.

"Just more Indian humor," Red Crow explained with a grin.

"Leonard's going to teach us how Indians really do things," Jack said. "He's even going to show us how to do a real rain dance."

"A rain dance?" I said. "Isn't that a waste of time? I mean, this is Seattle."

"Who do you think's responsible for all the rain?" Leonard flashed a big smile.

For the next couple of weeks, whenever the Minotauk met, Leonard Red Crow was there. He taught us to rain dance, shoot bows and arrows, throw tomahawks, paddle canoes, and tie Indian knots. Mom even silk-screened some sweatshirts with "The Noble Minotauk" written on them.

I don't know how it happened, but we actually got pretty good at some of the stuff. After a while, we were hitting the bull's-eye with our arrows, and we could throw tomahawks straight into trees. We must have become good at the rain dance because one afternoon in Stanley Park, while we were practicing it, we heard a *BOOM!* and then a *CRACK!* It started to thunder and lightning. The next thing we knew, it was pouring!

What's weird is that I became so interested in the Indian stuff that I almost forgot how dorky the Indian Guides were. And I spent so much time with Jack I almost forgot that I was trying to get rid of him.

Then one morning, when I came down to the kitchen, Jack was already there, taking out the fruit, yogurt, and granola for breakfast.

"Listen, Ben," Jack said, "I have to ask you a favor." He looked at me hopefully.

"Oh yeah?" I eyed him warily as I took a bowl and poured some granola into it.

"Chet Bronski and I . . . well, we've done a lot of talking," Jack said. "And he tells me Norm doesn't have many friends. He knows that a lot of kids his age go on sleep-overs, but he's never been invited to one."

"Do I *have* to?" I asked.

Jack looked surprised. "I thought you liked Norm."

"Well, he's okay, I guess."

"Then what's the problem?"

"Well, seeing him in Indian Guides is one thing," I tried to explain. "But having him sleep over . . . I don't know."

"Look, Norm's dad has helped me out a few times," Jack said. "I thought this would be a nice gesture. So please do me this one favor, okay?"

It was pretty amazing that I'd gotten to the point where I would even consider doing Jack a favor. I guess all that rain dancing and bow and arrow shooting we had done together had had some weird affect on me.

"What am I supposed to do with him?" I asked.

"I don't know," Jack said. "What do you do when Monroe comes over?"

"We play poker and watch dirty movies," I said sarcastically.

"Okay, then do the same thing with Norm," Jack said. "In fact, I'll join you."

Wasn't it weird? I'd even started talking in the same sarcastic way as him.

"Just think of all the good karma you'll rack up," Jack said. "You can probably get into heaven on this one deal alone."

I let out a big sigh to make sure he knew I considered this to be a favor of *major* proportions. "Okay. But hanging with a guy like that doesn't do so much for my reputation, you know?"

Jack nodded. "Yeah, we wouldn't want it getting around what a nice guy you are."

"Very funny." I made a face.

_T E N_

The night of the sleep-over, Jack set up a tepee on the roof of our building. And as a joke, Mom drew a big yellow happy face on it. Norm and I sat outside the tepee, wearing feathers and roasting marshmallows on a hibachi. I could see that the black sedan was parked down the street again. I still didn't think much about it, though.

"It was real nice of you to invite me to sleep over, Ben," he said.

"No sweat," I said. "Glad to do it."

"This is the first time I've ever been invited to stay over at someone's house."

"It's no big deal, Norm. Don't worry about it," I said.

Norm sort of grinned and then stared at his roasting marshmallow for a while. We talked about the upcoming canoe trip and camping trip that we both were going on with the Indian Guides. I couldn't think of anything else to say, but then Norm said, "Oh, I almost forgot. I brought you something."

He reached into the tent and took out a very cool fringed leather vest. It was made of really soft leather and had very intricate beadwork.

"This is for me?" I asked, amazed. "It must've cost you a fortune."

"Not really," Norm said. "I made it myself."

"No kidding?" I said. "All this beadwork must've taken forever."

"Well, it's not like I have much else to do," Norm said with a shrug. "Anyway, I thought you might like to have it."

I have to admit that I was a little uncertain about what was going on. I mean, it must have taken him months to make the vest, and, except for the Indian Guides, I hardly knew him.

"Listen, Norm," I said, "I have to be honest with you. I really don't get why you'd do something like this."

"Well, because I wanted to," Norm said simply. "And because we're part of the same tribe and everyting. I mean, if you don't like it, you can tell me. My feelings won't be hurt."

"Listen, I think this is really cool," I said. "Thanks a lot, Norm, really."

Norm smiled, and we sat there for a while more, grilling marshmallows in front of the tepee. It was fun while it lasted, but it got old pretty quick. Finally I turned to him and said, "I've got an idea. Do you want to bag this Indian stuff and go back to my room to play video games?"

"Would I ever!" Norm smiled.

"Let's do it," I said as we stood up, went through the roof door, and down to the loft.

"So what do you have?" Norm asked.

"I just got the new Subhumanoid Slaughterhouse Five Thousand," I said. "It's really cool but super-hard."

"I didn't even know it had come out," Norm gasped. "I'm still on the Subhumanoid Slaughterhouse Two Thousand."

We started to climb the stairs up to my room. "The Two Thousand's for twerps," I said. "The Five Thousand's better. You know the subhumanoid commander, Gackmo?"

"Yeah?" Norm didn't sound sure.

"Well, when you kill him his head explodes like a giant zit," I said with a chuckle.

"Cool!" Norm said, laughing.

The next schoolday, I wore the Indian vest to school. I was opening my locker when Monroe came up.

"Uh, Ben?" he said.

"Hey, Mon," I said.

"Mind if I ask what you're wearing?"

"This? It's an Indian vest. What's it look like?" I said.

"It looks like Gackmo the subhumanoid's head exploded all over your shirt," Monroe said, pointing at the beads. "What are those things?"

"These happen to be authentic Indian beads," I said proudly.

Monroe studied me for a moment. "Don't you think you're getting a little wrapped up in this Indian stuff?"

"I knew you were going to get on my case," I said. "But you know something? The Indian Guide stuff's not as bad as we thought. I've learned a lot of cool things."

"Like what?" Monroe asked.

"Like how to shoot a bow and arrow and throw a tomahawk," I said. "Can you do that?"

Monroe shook his head.

"Well, now I can." I beamed.

Monroe nodded. "Great. That should come in real handy the next time you go buffalo hunting."

I closed my locker, and we started walking toward class.

"And get this," I said. "Next weekend we're going on a big canoe trip. White-water rapids and everything. It's going to be great."

"Hey! Come on, guys, not again!" Down the hall someone was pleading for mercy. Two big kids were trying to push Norm into his locker again.

"Well, well," Monroe said. "Looks like Norm's getting crammed in his locker again. See what dressing up like an Indian gets you?"

I stopped to see if that was really what was happening. Then I felt Monroe tug my arm.

"Come on, we're going to be late," he said.

But I didn't budge. Instead, I started down the hall toward Norm.

"Where are you going?" Monroe asked.

"I'm going to help him," I said.

"You're going to get your butt kicked is what you're going to do." Then Monroe said under his breath, "I can't watch this. See you later, Ben."

Monroe took off down another corridor, and I went up to the guys who were stuffing Norm into his locker. They were both bigger than me.

"Excuse me," I said to the big kids. "What do you think you're doing?"

One of the guys turned and glowered at me. "You talking to us, punk?"

"You mean you're so stupid you can't tell when I'm talking to you?" I asked.

Now the other guy turned. "What'd you say?"

"I said let him go or you'll be wearing your butt for a hat," I said.

I never realized how much room there was inside a locker.

About twenty seconds later the locker door closed,

and I was in the dark. The cool metal of the locker wall pressed against my cheek, elbows, and knees.

From inside the locker next to mine, Norm said, "Ben, I really appreciate the effort."

"I thought it'd work," I said, shifting my hips around to find a more comfortable position. "You know, it's not so bad in here."

"Yeah," Norman said. "It's amazing how you get used to it after a while."

E L E V E N

The morning of the big canoe trip, Jack said he had to run over to his office for a couple of hours to take care of some business. He promised he'd be back in time to leave on our trip.

I packed up my stuff and walked over to the parking lot where the Indian Guides were meeting. The fathers were tightening the straps on the canoes, which were all tied to a trailer behind Chet's car. The kids were sitting on a log watching them and talking.

"Hey, Ben, where's Jack?" Norm asked as I sat down on the log.

"He had to go to the office," I said. "But he promised he'd be here soon."

We sat around while the fathers checked to make sure they had all the food and equipment. Then Chet came over.

"Okay, Guides," he said, slapping his hands together, "everybody ready for the big canoe trip?"

"Yeah!" we all shouted.

"We'll be going over a lot of white-water rapids," he said.

"Yeah!"

"Some of us might fall out and get torn to bits!"

"Yeah!"

"By man-eating salmon!"

"Yeah!"

Chet smiled and nodded. "Okay then. Let's get going."

I looked back up the street, but there was no sign of Jack's white truck. "What about Jack?" I asked.

"Oh, right," Chet said. "We're going to wait for him. Did he say what time he'd be here?"

"By noon," I said. "He promised."

"Well, if he promised, then he'll be here," Chet said.

We waited. Noon came and went. No, I thought, Jack wouldn't break his promise. Not Jack. Not after everything we'd done together over the past month.

Chet and the other fathers stood around Chet's van talking and checking their wristwatches. It was obvious that they were trying to decide whether or not to leave without Jack. Finally, Chet nodded and turned toward us.

"Okay, guys, come on," he said, slapping his hands together again. "Load up. Time to go."

The other kids got up and headed for the van. Norm stood up and glanced back at me, looking like he wasn't sure what to do.

"Go on," I said.

He shrugged and nodded sadly, then turned toward the van. Meanwhile, Chet stood by the log and scuffed his foot against the ground. "Look, Ben," he said reluctantly. "Silver Fox won't let us wait any longer."

"Yeah, sure," I said. "I understand."

"I mean, Jack's got an important job," Chet said. "So I'm sure whatever's keeping him has got to be pretty important, too."

"Yeah." I nodded, but inside I didn't agree. Jack should have been here. He'd *promised*! I didn't know how it happened, but I had reached the point where I counted on him.

"Why don't you come along with Norm and me?" Chet said. "You can sit in the middle of the canoe, and we'll all take turns paddling. How about it?"

I could see myself, the only Little Guide on the trip without a Big Guide.

"No thanks, Mr. Bronski," I said. "I don't feel much like going, anyway. I was just going along because Jack likes canoeing."

"You sure?" he asked.

"Yeah," I said, getting up. "You guys go ahead and have a great time. I'll be okay."

Chet nodded and headed back to the van. Then he stopped and turned. "Hey, Ben!"

I looked up, and he shouted, "Hey-ha-wa-ya!"

I forced a smile on my face and watched as he got into the van. As he started to drive away with everyone inside, he rolled down his window and waved.

Thinking that there still was a slight chance that Jack's car was going to come racing up the street, I took my time walking home. I imagined that he'd be full of excuses about why he was late. I'd tell him it was no problem, I'd jump in the car, and we'd race after Chet and the other kids. But when I got to our building, there was still no sign of him. Jack had broken his promise. He was just like my dad.

I walked into the apartment and dropped my bag. Mom looked surprised to see me.

"What are you doing back so early?" she asked. "Where's Jack?"

"He didn't show," I said.

Mom's forehead wrinkled. "What do you mean?"

"I mean, he promised he'd be there, and he never showed up," I said, flopping down onto the living room couch. "So the other guys went without me."

Mom came over and sat down next to me. "Oh, baby, I'm so sorry. I'm sure there's a good explanation." She tried to stroke my head, but I moved away.

"Yeah, and you really want to know what that

explanation is?" I said. "He didn't show because he found something better to do."

"No, Jack wouldn't do something like that," Mom said.

"Just like you knew Dad wouldn't do something like that," I muttered.

Mom looked hurt. "That's not fair," she said.

"Maybe not, but it's true," I said angrily. "You said, 'Go ahead, make an effort,' So I did. I even gave the stupid Indian Guides a chance, and look what it got me."

"I know you're upset," Mom said, "but there could be a million logical reasons why he didn't come."

And then there was a knock on the door. It was Jack. His hair was plastered to his head, and water was dripping off his soaking-wet suit.

"Jack, what happened?" Mom gasped, rising off the couch.

"I, uh, had car trouble," Jack said. "Nothing to worry about. Just a little problem with the brakes."

"Why are you so wet?" Mom asked.

"Oh, am I?" Jack said, pretending he hadn't noticed. "Well, I ran all the way home. Guess I worked up a sweat."

Then he saw me and started into the living room.

"You better get out of those clothes," Mom said behind him. "You'll catch pneumonia. I'll get you a towel."

She went into the bedroom. Jack knelt down next

to me and gazed steadily at me. "I'm really sorry I missed the canoe trip, Ben."

I nodded but refused to look at him.

"You didn't want to go without me?" Jack asked.

"It takes two people to paddle a canoe," I said. "In case you forgot."

"I had car trouble, Ben," Jack said. "It's not like I missed the trip on purpose. I wanted to be there, I really did."

"Yeah, right." I didn't believe him for a moment. He could have left the car in the garage and taken a cab with time to spare. I got up and headed for the stairs to my room. I'd had enough of his lies.

In my room, I sat down in front of the TV and started playing Subhumanoid Slaughterhouse Five Thousand. I knew downstairs Mom and Jack were talking about what happened, but for once I wasn't interested in listening.

After a while I heard someone outside my door. I felt myself get tense.

"Ben?" It was Jack. "Think I could talk to you for a second?"

I didn't answer. Jack pushed the door open a little and stepped into the room. He was wearing a robe now. Once again he told me how sorry he was that he'd missed the trip. I told him not to worry about it, that I didn't really want to go anyway. Then I went back to playing Subhumanoid Slaughterhouse. I hoped he'd just leave me alone, but he didn't. He crossed his arms and just stood there.

"Look, Ben," he said. "I know you're mad at me. And I know you have no reason in the world to believe me, but I swear I'm going to make it up to you. You know there's still that camping trip coming up?"

"What about it?" I said.

"Well, I'm giving my word," Jack said. "Nothing's going to stop me from going with you. We're going to have the best time we ever had. I promise. Okay?"

"Yeah, sure." I stared at the game and watched the subhumanoids bash each other. If Jack only knew how many times I'd heard those words before.

"Okay, great." Jack left my room. It didn't matter what he did or said. We were back to square one. He was Jack the jerk again, and this time I wasn't going to change my mind.

Since his dad left, Ben has learned to enjoy doing special things with his mom.

Jack—the new "jerk" in his mom's life—whips up a gourmet breakfast for Ben.

Ben and Jack join a father-and-son group called the Indian Guides.

Jack competes in a traditional grapefruit-carrying game with Chet Bronski.

Jack tries to explain to Ben's mom that he wants to quit the Indian Guides.

Ben learns some pointers in archery from a colleague of Jack's, Leonard Red Crow.

Ben and Jack join Chet and Norman Bronski as they paddle upstream on their big camping trip.

In camp the first night, Jack amuses his fellow campers with a "traditional" story.

From a hiding place, Ben and Jack spy on the hit men who have followed them.

Jack explains to Ben and the other fathers that they'll have to leave and go find help.

Ben and Jack prepare to defend themselves against the hit men.

Trapped by the hit men, Ben and Jack try to talk their way out of the jam.

Jack leads the men away after he and Ben manage to out-smart the bad guys.

Ben is all smiles the day "Jack the jerk" becomes . . . his new dad.

T W E L V E

Then something weird happened. A couple of mornings later, I got up and Jack was still home. Usually he went to his office before I came down for breakfast. I asked him what was going on, and he said he was taking a little time off. As usual, I didn't think I was getting the whole story.

He stayed around the loft for the rest of that week. His white truck was nowhere in sight. I even asked Mom what was going on, but she just said Jack had been on a special project and now he was going to take a break for a while.

Then the Indian Guides camping trip rolled around. Jack and I joined the other Guides at Chet's house and drove up into the mountains. When we got there we left the van at the ranger station, then started to hike through the woods to the campsite. Jack was in a really good mood. I guess he was happy because he thought he was proving to me that he could keep his word. But frankly, I wasn't impressed.

"Hey, Chet," he called out as we walked along a small tree-lined stream. "How about a sing-along?"

"Good idea," Chet said. "What do you want to sing?"

"How about 'Louie, Louie'?" Jack said.

"Point of order," said Red. "I believe it's 'Louie, Lou-eye,' and I don't think the boys would know the lyrics."

"That's the great thing about the song," Jack said. "*No one* knows the lyrics. You can just mumble any nonsense you want, and it'll sound fine."

The next thing I knew, they started singing that dumb song, making up all these idiotic lyrics. Jack kept looking at me like he wanted me to join in, but I just rolled my eyes.

Finally we got to the campground. The other kids helped their fathers put up their tepees, but I just didn't feel like helping Jack. Instead I played with my pocket video game while Jack spread all the parts of the tepee on the ground and tried to figure out how to put it together.

"Hey, Ben," he said. "Look at all this stuff. I'm sure glad this is a single. Can you imagine trying to put up a two-bedroom tepee?"

I didn't know what he was talking about. "No, I can't," I said.

Jack just stood there with his hands on his hips and sighed. "That was my subtle way of asking for help, Ben."

"You'll have to be more obvious," I told him. "I'm just a kid, remember? I don't get subtleties."

"Okay, fine," Jack said impatiently. "I'll make it more obvious. Everyone else has their tepee up, and ours is lying on the ground. How about giving me a hand?"

"No," I said. "My back's sore."

"Fine," Jack, replied. "I'll get someone else to help me." He turned to the others. "Hey, Lloyd, think you could help me?"

Lloyd, the guy who never spoke, came over. He and Jack tried to get the tepee up, but it kept falling down. The other Guides started to gather around and laugh. Finally, Jack climbed up into a tree and lowered some ropes to tie some branches to the top of the tepee to keep it from falling. Everyone applauded. Everyone except me.

Later on we had a campfire, and we all sat around it eating franks and beans for dinner. Then we stared at the flames, too tired and full to do anything else. Chet was wearing his Indian chief headdress. He looked up at the star-filled sky.

"It doesn't get much better than this, does it?" he asked.

The other Guides murmured in agreement.

"You know, Guides," Chet said, "there are more stars in the heavens than there are grains of sand on every beach in the world."

"You think maybe on one of those stars there's a bunch of fathers and sons sitting around a campfire, basking in the warm glow of friendship?" asked Red.

Then Lloyd, the guy who never talked, made some gestures to his son, Darryl.

"My dad says that if there are, they probably all have big heads and three eyes," Darryl said.

"Hey," Jack said. "That gives me an idea. Anyone interested in a story?"

Everyone nodded. Jack asked Chet if he could borrow his Indian headdress. It was strange to think that I was once totally convinced that Jack would hate being an Indian Guide.

"Okay," Jack said, straightening the headdress on his head, "this is a very old Indian legend passed from generation to generation. Either that or I saw it on an episode of *F Troop*. Remember that show where all the Indians would . . . talk . . . like . . . this?"

"Real Native Americans don't talk like that," said Hank, Red's son.

"Squatting Dog know this," Jack said, crossing his arms. "Use only for comic effect . . . entertain Minotauk."

So, talking like a TV Indian, Jack continued with his story. "Many moon ago, was young Lakota guide homeboy name Pain in Butt, named by father,

64

Take Too Long on Can."

Everyone laughed uproariously. I just smirked. It was funny, but not *that* funny.

"One day Take Too Long on Can run off with pretty nurse named Gives Terrific Sponge Bath," Jack said. "This very sad for Pain in Butt's mother, Cleans a Lot. She stop dusting tepee. Never take out garbage. Plenty bad medicine. Years go by. Pain in Butt grow into young guide, take care of Cleans a Lot. Their life together very happy. . . ."

I had a feeling I knew where this was headed. I was embarrassed that Jack was talking about my personal life.

"Then one day Cleans a Lot bring home incredibly handsome Lakota warrior named Looks So Good. She say, 'Pain in Butt, this Looks So Good. I have decided marry him.' "

Everyone laughed out loud, and some of the Guides even glanced at me. I felt my face turn red. That was it. Tomorrow I was going to "accidentally" push Jack off a cliff.

"Pain in Butt not like Looks So Good from get go. Not like way him ruin happy life Pain in Butt have with Cleans a Lot. So he do everything he can to make Looks So Good look so bad. Pour glue in moccasin. Put iguana in underwear. Order ten pizza, have delivered to Looks So Good tepee. Run up big bills calling 1-900 numbers."

"Sound like Pain in Butt could use a bit of discipline," said Red. "Maybe trip to woodshed."

"No, no, Silver Fox," said Jack. "Pain in Butt no need discipline. Him just make mistake all Little Guides make. Him not trust Big Guide. Him think all Big Guide the same. One disappoint, all disappoint."

"But this not always so," said Chet. "Pain in Butt need learn trust."

I couldn't believe what dorks these guys were being.

"Good medicine, Running Horse." Jack nodded at Chet. "But trust funny thing. No matter how hard one try, sooner or later one bound to mess up. Break trust. Not mean to."

Then Jack went back to his regular voice. "Now, what can Guides learn from this story?"

"The most important thing," said Red, "is Little Guides must never call 1-900 numbers without their parents' permission."

"Good point, Silver Fox," said Jack. "But you're way off as usual. What do you think, Chief Running Horse?"

"Huh?" It was pretty obvious Chet had been caught off guard. "Is it the golden rule thing?"

"Nice try, Running Horse," said Jack, "but not even close."

Now Lloyd, the guy who never spoke, jumped up and acted something out.

"Sorry, Lloyd," Jack said, shaking his head. Then he turned toward the kids. "Maybe Squatting Dog will have better luck with the Little Guides. What do you think, Dark Eagle?"

"I think it means you have to learn to trust people," Norm said. "Even if sometimes they disappoint you."

"Very good! Dark Eagle's hit the nail on the head!" Jack said. Then he turned and looked at me. "And Little Wing? What do *you* think?"

I knew he was going to put me on the spot, and it made me mad. I got up. "I think maybe Looks So Good should've been called Minds His Own Business."

Then I went into the tepee.

THIRTEEN

The next morning I was up early, and Chet asked me to go down to the creek to fill the canteens. I took all the canteens and headed over to the creek. Suddenly I heard this voice say, "Gotcha! I told you I could do it!"

It didn't sound like any of the Indian Guides, so I snuck through the brush to take a look. Standing in the middle of the stream was this mean-looking man wearing a black suit and holding up a fish. The strange thing was, he looked vaguely familiar. Two other guys in suits stood on the edge of the creek, watching.

"You're not going to believe it," the guy in the black suit was saying to the other two men, "but this is the first time I fished in my entire life. I could actually learn to like this. Hey, Murray, maybe after we knock off this Sturges guy we could come back and try this again."

Knock off this Sturges guy? I'd watched enough TV to know that was mobster talk for killing someone. And suddenly I remembered where I'd seen the guy in the black suit. He was one of the men who was always sitting around in that black sedan near my building. I remembered Mom talking about how Jack had sent some bad guys to jail for a long time. Maybe those criminals had some friends who were looking for revenge!

I quietly backed away from the bushes and then hurried back to the campsite. Jack was starting a fire for breakfast. He looked up and waved. "Hey, Ben." But then he must have seen the look on my face, because he stopped smiling. "What's going on?"

"There are some mean-looking guys in suits down by the creek fishing," I said as I gasped for breath. "One of them said they came up here to kill you."

Jack's eyes widened. "Where are they?"

"I'll show you."

I quickly led Jack back down to the creek, and we hid in the bushes. The guy was still standing in the middle of the creek, waiting to grab another fish, and his friends were still standing at the creek's edge. Each of them was holding a fish.

"Come on, Tony," one of them said, "enough with this fishing."

"Just one more," Tony begged. "I'm getting really good at this."

"If you were as good at arranging car accidents," said the other guy, "Sturges would be dead by now, and we wouldn't be standing around in the forest like Robin Hood and his merry men."

I felt Jack's hand close around my arm, and he quietly led me away. As soon as we were out of earshot, we started to jog back to the campsite.

"What accident were they talking about?" I asked.

"The other day." Jack huffed as we ran.

"I thought you just had some car trouble," I said.

"Well, I did," he said. "I just didn't tell you how *much* car trouble."

"So how much was it?" I asked.

Of course, Mr. Cool U.S. Attorney didn't want to tell me.

"Aw, come on, tell me," I said.

"Those guys cut my brake lines," Jack finally said. "I went right into the bay."

"Why didn't you tell us?" I asked.

"I didn't want you or your mom to get upset," Jack said.

"Well, you should've told me," I said. "I thought that car-trouble story was just an excuse to get out of going on the canoe trip. If you'd told me the truth, I would have believed you."

"I'm sorry, Ben," Jack said. "I thought I was doing the right thing."

"Well, next time someone tries to kill you, let me in on it, okay?" I said.

"You got it." When we arrived back at the campsite, Jack went over to Chet and took him aside. "Hey, Chet, I need you to do something for me. Don't ask a lot of questions, but three guys followed me up here. They're sort of after me."

"What do you mean?" Chet asked. Now Red and Lloyd came over.

"It's a revenge thing," Jack explained. "I sent one of their friends to prison for a long time."

"What do you want us to do?" Chet asked.

"You and the boys work your way back down to the ranger station and get help. I'll take some arrows and tomahawks and lead these guys farther up the mountain until you get back."

"I don't know, Jack," Chet said, scratching his head. "Maybe we should stay around here and help you."

Lloyd put up his fists like he was ready to fight, and Red said, "I must concur with Silent Thunder on that point, Jack. There's eight of us. I'd say the odds were distinctly in our favor."

"That's real nice of you guys," Jack said. "But they're after me, and they're very well trained at killing people. It's too dangerous for us to stay together. Now get going."

Despite Jack's warning, Lloyd and Red were obviously disappointed, but Chet understood.

"Okay, but we'll be back as fast as we can," Chet said, turning to the kids. "Little Guides, get ready to move out!"

That's when I realized Jack expected me to go down to the ranger station. There was no way I was leaving him.

"That means you, too, Ben," Jack said.

"No way," I protested.

"You're not staying," Jack said.

"But I can help," I said.

"You can be more help by making sure the others get back down okay," Jack said. "Now get on out of here. I mean it!"

"But . . . ," I tried to argue.

Jack pointed a finger sternly at me. "Go!"

I turned away reluctantly and went to join the others.

"Hey, Ben," Jack said behind me. I spun around hopefully, but he just waved. "Thanks, anyway," he said. "I appreciate the offer."

Then Jack yelled to Chet, pretending he was just going off to scout some stuff while the rest of us took a different trail. Chet yelled back that we'd probably beat him to the top. It was all just an act in case those bad guys were watching and listening.

Jack disappeared into the woods, and Chet started to lead us back down the mountain. "Okay, everyone," he yelled. "Stay in line and don't get lost. Let's move fast!"

Everyone started to jog down the trail. I made sure I was the last in line. As soon as we came to a sharp curve on the path through thick trees, I made a quick turn and disappeared into the brush.

A moment later I was climbing back up the mountain. There was no way I was going to leave Jack alone with those killers.

F O U R T E E N

I got back to the campsite and then continued up the way I'd seen Jack go. He couldn't have been that far ahead. I climbed up through the trees and rocks, keeping my eyes peeled for Jack *and* for the bad guys.

Yeee-achoooo!

The sudden sound almost made me jump out of my skin. What kind of animal made a noise that sounded like a sneeze? None that I knew of. Then maybe it *was* a sneeze. Allergies, I thought . . . Jack.

"Gesundheit," I said in a whisper.

"Ben!" It was Jack.

I pushed through some brush and found him lying on the ground. His right leg was wedged painfully between a fallen log and a big rock.

Jack stared up at me. "What're you doing here?"

"I came back to help you."

"I don't need any help."

He *had* to be kidding. "Oh, really? What were you planning to do when those guys found you trapped under this log? Lie there and pretend to be a slug?" I asked.

"Exactly," Jack replied. "Now get out of here before you blow my cover."

"You can't tell me what to do," I said. "You're not my father."

Jack shook his head and sighed. "I knew you'd say that someday."

I wasn't going to stand around gabbing with him. Instead I got my shoulder under the log and pushed with all my might. I managed to move it just enough for Jack to slide his leg out. He got up slowly and winced in pain.

"How's the leg?" I asked.

"Except for the throbbing pain, great," he said sarcastically, and then he grimaced.

"I guess that means we're not going to outrun them," I said, looking at the forest around us and hoping they weren't close by.

"What do you think we should do?" Jack asked.

"We better try to slow them down until the others get back with help," I said.

"Do you have a plan?" he asked. "Or are we just going to wing it?"

"You know what Leonard Red Crow once told me?" I said. "When you need an answer, just listen to nature and the answer will come."

"How do you know that wasn't just more of his Indian humor?" Jack asked.

"Just listen," I said.

"Okay, I'm listening," he said, cupping his ears with his hands. I guess he couldn't hear what I heard because he added, "Ask nature to speak up, will you. I can't hear anything."

"Shush," I said.

Buuuuuzzzzzzzzzzzzz . . .

"You hear it?" I asked, pointing at a tree nearby. At the end of a long thin branch was a huge beehive with hundreds of bees swarming around.

Jack grinned. "Well, thank you, Leonard Red Crow."

It didn't take me long to cut through the branch with a small camp knife. We made a few other preparations, like sharpening tomahawks and arrows. Then Jack left some Indian beads on the trail to lead the thugs in our direction.

Jack and I huddled together behind a big tree.

"You ready?" I whispered.

"Yeah," he said.

"How's the leg?" I asked.

"Hurts, but I'll be okay. So, uh, shouldn't we high-five or something first?"

I gave him a look that said, Don't act like a dork.

Jack nodded. "Right. No fiving."

Suddenly, in the woods below us, we could hear the voices of the thugs coming closer as they climbed up the trail.

"Hey, here's some more of that beaded junk," one of them was saying. "They must be around here somewhere."

Jack gave me a nudge and a wink. I stepped onto the trail with a bow and arrow and whistled. Two of the guys appeared. The third must've split off from them.

"Hey, look!" The guy in the black suit pointed at me. "It's his kid! What's he doin'?"

"I think he's gonna shoot us with his bow and arrow," the other one said with a grin.

"Ooooh, I'm really scared," the first one laughed.

Zip! I let the arrow fly high over their heads.

"Aw, he missed," one of them said.

It was true that I'd missed *them.* But I did hit the beehive that we'd hung just over the trail. That made the bees really mad. They started to buzz like crazy. The thugs were looking up at the hive when . . . *Whooosh!* Jack hurled his tomahawk at the branch holding it.

Whack! The tomahawk cut clean through the branch.

"Ahhhhhhhhhh!" Both bad guys screamed as the beehive with all its bees crashed down on them. The next thing we knew, they took off down the trail

screaming like crazy. Each had a cloud of irate bees around his head.

Jack and I joined up again.

"Good shot, Little Wing," he said.

"You too, Squatting Dog," I said.

Jack cringed. "You know, we really ought to think about changing my name."

"Yeah," said a voice behind us. "How's about Dead Meat?"

Jack and I spun around. It was the third tough guy, and he was aiming a rifle at us!

FIFTEEN

The man with the rifle was named Joey. He held the rifle on us until the other two men came back. The one with the black suit was named Tony. The third guy was named Murray. Tony and Murray had big red welts from bee stings on their faces and hands.

They obviously weren't happy.

"I'm gonna kill them right now!" Tony shouted, staggering toward us and pulling out a long thin knife with a black handle.

"Hold it!" Joey shouted. "Remember, we've got to make it look like an accident."

"How're you going to do that?" Murray asked.

Joey pointed farther up the mountain. At first I didn't see anything. Then I noticed a dark opening in the face of the mountain a few hundred yards above us.

"What is it?" Tony asked.

"An abandoned mine," Joey said. "And that's just what we need."

It took them a while to get us to the opening of the mine because Jack was limping pretty slowly. Finally we made it up there.

"You stand over there," Joey said, pointing to a spot near the entrance of the mine. Then Tony and Murray packed explosives around the mine's entrance and laid out a fuse.

Although I was trying my best not to show it, I was scared silly. I mean, these guys weren't fooling around. They actually planned to *kill* us. My teeth were chattering with fear. For some reason, Jack didn't come across that nervous. I figured he had to be either really stupid or really brave. And I was pretty sure he wasn't stupid.

"You know, Joey," Jack said, "even though you're a semiliterate demi-moron, I expected something better than this from you."

Joey's forehead wrinkled. "What are you talkin' about?"

"Come on," Jack said. "The old 'seal 'em up in an abandoned mine and make it look like a cave-in' gag?"

"What's wrong with it?" Joey asked.

At first I thought Jack was crazy to taunt him like that. Then I thought maybe I understood what he was doing. I even joined in.

"For starters, it's totally boring," I said. "It shows a complete lack of imagination."

"I suppose you could think of something better?" Joey asked, sticking out his lower lip.

"Without even trying," Jack replied. "You could hurl us off a cliff onto jagged rocks."

"That's not better," Joey said.

"Yeah," I said. "Or if you were *really* clever, which you're not, you'd wrap us up in wet rawhide. Then as it dried it would mash up our bones and squeeze our internal organs out through our orifices like a tube of toothpaste."

The next thing I knew, Joey, Tony, and Murray had stopped what they were doing and were staring at me. Even Jack was staring at me. They all looked completely grossed out by what I was saying.

"Hey," I said, "I saw it on the evening news."

Jack blinked and shook his head. Then he turned to Joey. "Listen, Joey, can I come with you? I don't want to get trapped in a mine with this kid."

"I know what you mean, Sturges," Joey said. "This kid is sick. If I wasn't planning to kill the two of you, I'd have suggested you get him psychiatric help. Murray, light the fuse quick, before this little demento gets any more ideas."

Tony shoved us into the mine, and Murray lit the fuse. Joey held the rifle on us in case we tried to escape.

"Bye-bye, Sturges," he said with a chuckle. "Bye-bye, kid."

"J-J-Jack . . . ," I stammered as we backed away from the entrance and into the darkness of the cave. My teeth were chattering again. Even if we didn't get killed in the blast or cave-in, we would be left to starve to death in the dark.

"Don't worry, Ben," Jack said. "It's going to be okay."

"How do *you* know?" I asked.

"Well, the truth is, I don't," Jack said. "But I've always believed that good would triumph over evil. I guess that's why I'm a prosecutor and not a defense lawyer."

"What are you—" Before I could finish the sentence, I was interrupted by a *zip!* It sounded like an arrow. The next thing I knew, it hit the fuse, cutting it in half and stopping the flame. Everyone turned to see Lloyd, the guy who didn't talk, holding a bow and arrow and grinning. Then he started jumping around, gesturing wildly.

"What the heck is this?" Joey sputtered. "Charades? I hate charades."

"He says throw down your weapons," Jack interpreted for Lloyd. "Otherwise, he will turn you into large, stupid-looking pincushions."

Joey glared hard at Jack. "Did he really say 'stupid-looking'?"

"Well, not really," Jack admitted while smiling. "I added that."

Tony nodded dubiously. "Yeah, right. Like we're going to surrender to one lunatic with a bow and arrow. Murray, put a bullet in his head, quick."

But when Murray reached into his jacket for his gun, someone said, "Excuse me. Point of order."

The thugs turned around and looked up. I could only imagine that Red must've been standing above the mine entrance.

"I believe it is illegal to possess firearms in a state park," Red informed them. "As a duly authorized representative of the Department of Motor Vehicles, a state agency, I'm going to have to confiscate your weapons."

"Now there are two of them," Joey groaned, shaking his head in wonder. "I guess I'm supposed to be *really* scared."

"Make that three," a voice said. We turned to see Chet step out of the woods and aim a bow and arrow at them.

"Four!" Norman stepped out of the woods with another bow and arrow.

"Five!" Darryl appeared.

"Six!" Now Hank appeared.

The mobsters were completely surrounded. Murray turned to Joey. "What do we do?" he asked.

Joey rolled his eyes in disbelief. "We got guns. They got little bows and arrows. What do you think we do?"

Murray started to pull his gun. Tony took out his knife.

"Okay, Guides," Chet shouted. "Let them have it!"

Zip! Zip! Zip! Zip! Four arrows instantly pinned Tony to a tree.

"Hey-ha-wa-ya!" Red jumped down from the mine entrance.

Whomp! He slammed into Murray, smashing him against a big rock.

"This is ridiculous!" Joey muttered, raising the rifle and aiming it at Chet.

Jack headed out of the cave, limping as fast as he could on his bad leg. He ran up behind Joey and yanked the rifle away.

"I don't think so, Joey." Jack grabbed him by the shirt and pulled him close. "Now, you little piece of lint! Apologize to Ben for making me break my promise to take him canoeing."

"What are you talking about?" Joey gasped.

"Just do it!" Jack shouted angrily, and shook him like a big doll.

"Okay, okay." Joey looked at me. "I'm sorry, Ben."

"Was that good enough?" Jack asked me.

"Yeah." I nodded.

"All right." Jack shoved Joey toward Red. "Hey, Red, add this piece of garbage to the pile."

Jack tossed the rifle to him, and Red held it on the three guys.

"Okay, you dirtbags," Red said. "Don't get smart with me. I got the gun."

Jack and I were dusting ourselves off when Chet and Lloyd came over.

"You guys okay?" Chet asked.

"Couldn't be better," Jack said. "Thanks for coming back."

"We didn't have much choice," Chet said. "If we'd really tried to find that ranger station, we would have gotten lost."

"And more important, we're Indian Guides," said Lloyd. "Indian Guides always stick together."

Lloyd walked away. Jack and I both were stunned.

"Wait a minute," Jack said. "I thought Lloyd couldn't talk."

"Oh, no, he can talk," Chet said. "He just doesn't do it unless he has something really important to say."

Jack smiled. Then we went over to the others, who were tying up the three guys, using all the Indian knots Leonard Red Crow had taught us.

"You know something, Ben," Jack said as we walked. "These Guides are the weirdest bunch of guys I've ever met. But I like them."

"I like them, too," I said.

Jack smiled. "I want to thank *you* for coming back, too. That was a very brave thing to do." He patted me on the back. He sounded really touched.

"Well, I couldn't just let them kill you," I said. "After all, my mom wants to keep you around for a while."

Jack studied me for a moment.

"And, uh, I guess I do, too," I added.

Jack nodded and started to limp back along the trail to the camp. Suddenly I realized I had a question for him.

"Hey," I said, "if you *knew* somebody was trying to kill you, why did you still come on this trip?"

Jack glanced over his shoulder to make sure we were out of earshot. "Well, Ben, to tell you the truth, I was hoping they'd miss me and get Red by accident." I knew he was kidding.

"Oh, I see . . ." I played along. "Then it *wasn't* because you didn't want to break your promise to come on this trip," I said.

"Of course not," Jack said with a smirk. "What do I look like? A moron?" He limped along a few steps more. "Hey, would you mind if I leaned on you? My leg's killing me."

S I X T E E N

A few weeks later, Jack and I walked home from the beach. His leg was better by then. Jack was carrying the plastic bucket filled with stuff we had collected for the collage.

"So, Ben," he said, "as long as we're buddies now . . . We *are* buddies now, right?"

"I suppose," I said.

"Good. Because there's something I want to talk to you about. It's a little difficult for me, because I'm a grown man and you're only eleven." He sounded nervous.

"You're going to ask for my mother's hand in marriage, aren't you?" I guessed.

Jack did a double take and just smiled at me. "Are you *sure* you're only eleven?" he asked.

"Want to see my driver's license?" I said with a grin.

"It's all right, I believe you," Jack said. "So how about it? Is it okay with you if I marry your mother?"

"What if I say no?" I asked.

Jack shook his head slowly. "You're going to play this for all it's worth, aren't you?"

"Well, Jack," I said, "the way I figure it, I'm not going to have any *real* power until I'm at least twenty-one. So I better enjoy this while I can."

"And how long will this last?" Jack asked.

"It all depends," I said as we got to our building and took the elevator up. "This is a big decision for a little person to make. She's my only mother. I can't let just *any* bozo marry her. There's a few things I need to know about you first."

Jack gave me a wary look. "My salary?"

"That's a start," I said, feeling very in control of the situation.

So he told me. It didn't sound like much.

"Is that *all* you make?" I asked, amazed.

"Hey, it's above minimum wage," Jack said as we went into the apartment. We stopped in front of the collage and started to fit into the picture the pieces we had just collected from the beach.

"Do you have any bad habits I should know about?" I asked.

"I drink milk straight from the carton," Jack said. "And sometimes after I use a spoon, I put it right back in the drawer," he added slyly.

"Do you at least wipe it off first?" I asked.

"Only if I feel like it," Jack answered.

"Any chance you might turn into a serial killer and boil our heads in acid?" I asked.

"Don't be ridiculous," Jack said. "I haven't done that in years."

We both smiled.

"So, do I pass?" Jack asked.

I shrugged. "You'll do, I guess."

"Can I tell your mother the good news?" he asked.

"Sure, go ahead," I said.

Jack stuck a piece of shell in the collage and then started to walk away. "By the way," he said, "about the boiling head thing . . . I lied."

Suddenly I noticed something about the collage and gasped. "Jack!"

"Oh, okay, I didn't lie," Jack said. He must've thought I was gasping about his last comment.

"No, no," I said. "Look at what you've done."

Jack stared at the collage and frowned. "What?"

"Step back about ten feet," I said.

Jack stepped back and blinked. Somehow, without realizing it, we had turned the collage into a perfect circle. The last piece Jack had put in place had completed it.

"Mom!" I yelled.

Mom came out of her bedroom. "What's the matter?"

"Look what Jack did," I said, pointing to the collage. Mom looked at it and started to smile.

"Well, what do you know." She put one arm around me and the other around Jack and hugged us both. "It's done."

SEVENTEEN

As you probably already figured out, I let Jack marry my mom. It seemed only fair, after what I put him through. We had the wedding on the roof. The Indian Guides came, along with some of Mom's artist friends and people from Jack's office. Jack and I wore tuxedos. I was the best man.

Jack and I still are Indian Guides. Last week, we made Jack our new chief. Next he says we're going to make reindeers out of clothespins.

I'd like to be able to tell you that we all lived happily ever after, but it's still too soon to tell. I guess the lesson to be learned from all this is that sometimes you just have to trust people and hope everything works out.

I mean, nothing's perfect, but you can still give it your best shot.

Also, it doesn't hurt to give dorks a chance.

And never laugh at people wearing traditional Indian costumes.

And finally, keep your locker neat. You never know when you might be spending time in it.